Instructions for my 5th Grade Self

PRAISE FOR *STORYSHARES*

"One of the brightest innovators and game-changers in the education industry."
– Forbes

"Your success in applying research-validated practices to promote literacy serves as a valuable model for other organizations seeking to create evidence-based literacy programs."

- Library of Congress

"We need powerful social and educational innovation, and Storyshares is breaking new ground. The organization addresses critical problems facing our students and teachers. I am excited about the strategies it brings to the collective work of making sure every student has an equal chance in life."
– Teach For America

"Around the world, this is one of the up-and-coming trailblazers changing the landscape of literacy and education."
- International Literacy Association

"It's the perfect idea. There's really nothing like this. I mean wow, this will be a wonderful experience for young people."   - Andrea Davis Pinkney, Executive Director, Scholastic

"Reading for meaning opens opportunities for a lifetime of learning. Providing emerging readers with engaging texts that are designed to offer both challenges and support for each individual will improve their lives for years to come. Storyshares is a wonderful start."
- David Rose, Co-founder of CAST & UDL

Instructions for my 5th Grade Self

Lisa Zhang

STORYSHARES

Story Share, Inc.
New York. Boston. Philadelphia

Storyshares
Story Share, Inc.
24 N. Bryn Mawr Avenue #340
Bryn Mawr, PA 19010-3304
www.storyshares.org

Inspiring reading with a new kind of book.

Interest Level: Middle School
Grade Level Equivalent: 5.0

9798885979207

Book design by Storyshares

Printed in the United States of America

Storyshares Presents

1

Outside the classroom, the weather is postcard perfect. The sky is an unbroken backdrop of blue. The radiant sun will wrap you in her warm and brilliant rays, but do not let it lull you to sleep. You must focus.

Let your eyes trail Mrs. Lou's arms as she scrawls an equation across the chalk-filled blackboard.

Someone will burp. Hold your breath! Do not giggle. Notice how the classroom grows silent—do not be the one to break it. As Mrs. Lou whirls around in her black turtleneck and velvet ankle-length skirt, fold your arms atop the desk, straighten your back, and, for God's sake, stop tapping your left foot!

"Karl?" Mrs. Lou drawls, "come up and solve this equation."

Notice how it isn't a question. It's a *command*. But you will feel your shoulders slouch. At least you were not the victim this time.

A warm breeze sweeps through the open windows and your baby hair glides across your forehead. You will risk a glance at the outer world. What a beautiful world it is! The trees move in harmony in the breeze.

Notice the flock of pigeons plunging across the sky. You envy them, their *freedom*. You will wish you could extend your limbs and float out the window, away from the classroom.

All of a sudden, some sixth sense will tell you that the room is unnaturally quiet. You will blink hard, twice, and snap back into focus. *Oh, crap*. Every pair of eyes, including Mrs. Lou's, is trained upon you. Further, Mrs. Lou is struggling to breathe. She looks like she will have a stroke. Wait... no. She is seething with anger. You will feel your chest tighten.

This will be your second strike this week. One more, and you'll end up on the Wall of Shame and be punished.

Mrs. Lou approaches your desk, her high heels clicking against the floor. *Why, Yijia, are you distracted yet again? Have you no respect for me? Your behavior and attitude are simply unbelievable!* On and on and on she will go.

Remind yourself that you have a routine for this. Take deep breaths and try to block out the noise by conjuring Dorothy—the beautiful, brilliant heroine from the *Wizard of Oz*. Her bravery will give you strength.

Close your eyes if it becomes unbearable, but not for too long. Mrs. Lou might think you are belittling her. Instead, make direct eye contact every three to five seconds. Don't stare too deep into those black pupils, though, or you may lose it and cry.

As Mrs. Lou pauses to replenish her lungs with oxygen, you will command your mind to prolong the moment before she starts again.

Then, you will yawn.

Oh no. *That* was a mistake. A terrible one. You will freeze, your lips still slightly parted.

Watch as Mrs. Lou's lower lip quivers. Your brain will start racing with possibilities: detention? Standing in the corner until lunch? Copying a poem twenty times?

"You will clean the bathroom after school." Mrs. Lou whispers in a voice you have never heard before. It will send chills down your spine.

Someone gasps. You will gape at your teacher, staring *into* her eyes this time. You will want to cry out against the injustice... but think, Yijia! Remember what your mother taught you: always consider the consequences before you act. Crying would only aggravate Mrs. Lou further. Instead, bite your tongue, hard. You will taste blood.

After you have made peace with your emotions, give the slightest nod. Keep your head down and shoulders slightly hunched as Mrs. Lou towers over you. Let your body language convey that you have learned your lesson. You will hear her clicking heels retreat. Even with the unthinkable task ahead, you will feel a wave of relief wash over you, your muscles loosening on their own accord.

When the bell rings, you will flee to your next class like the devil is chasing you.

2

Dreading the task ahead, you will act like the dead for the remainder of the school day, only awakening at the monotonous ding-dong of the dismissal bell. Notice how the faintest hint of a smile is starting to crawl on everyone's faces. Reiterate your hatred for Mrs. Lou.

Hide in the storage room until you hear the last set of footsteps fade out of earshot. Then, slip back out. Let yourself tiptoe amongst the shadows. You'd make an amazing thief, you will think to yourself mournfully, except that instead of stealing a golden crown off some sleeping beauty's head in a grand castle, you are on your way to the Hole, the not-so-endearing nickname for the restroom. Sigh noisily and curse Mrs. Lou again.

Take a bucket and a mop from the janitor's room. Fill the bucket with clean water. Dip the mop in, wring it, and murmur a quick prayer before you enter the innermost stall. Now, tip-toe around the perimeter and edge your way to the flushometer.

If you hear a funny squishy noise beneath your shoe, do not freeze. Your eyes will have the urge to wander, a natural instinct, but you must keep them trained to the opposite stall door. If you risk a glance downwards, you are done for: the endless surprises never fail to make you gag.

Once you're within range, grasp the handle, place one hand on top of the other, and give a little jump. After you hear the initial flushing die down, count to five, and push again.

You will feel your shoulders loosen: the worst part is over. Now, take the mop and wipe away at the floor while still keeping your eyes level. Avoid the corners if you can. That is janitor territory. Make your cautious exit when your arm muscles start to strain. Rinse the mop and watch the bucket become a bowl of brown mushy soup.

You will feel your stomach churn. Clasp your throat after gulping down some bile. Collapse against the stall door for support, and let your trembling hands reach into your jacket pocket. Like a miracle, you will find a handful of candy. Stuff as many as you can into your mouth and chew. Utilize those strong, healthy teeth that are the result of relentless parental supervision. Let the sweetness override the queasiness.

As black dots disappear from your vision, you will sigh and proceed to the next stall.

A century later, you will finally exit the last stall. Your prayer must have been heard; you made it through unscathed. You will hum to yourself, even waltz a little. All of a sudden, your shoe will lose its traction and squeal, knocking over the bucket of liquid. You will sense your neck muscles strain as you fall, powerless against gravity. Hands flailing, you will land on your back. *Oh no*. Check if any bones have cracked. Try moving your hands, arms, legs. You will feel dizzy. Is it from the fall or from the stench?

Wearily haul yourself to your feet. Your back is soaked, but you will be too stunned to even open your mouth. Be glad that nothing is going to come out.

Go ahead and trudge towards the sink. Wash your hands and arms with *clean* water. The rest will have to wait. Notice how your tartan collared shirt is stained a grizzly-bear brown.

Sink your teeth into your bottom lip and recall your favorite book, *The Wizard of Oz*, again. You are the good-hearted heroine, Dorothy, being held against your will in a foreign land (the bathroom, and it's not so foreign), wishing to return home. Of course there are trials along the way! But if Dorothy can make it through in one piece, so can you, Yijia. So, quit standing there like you are waiting to catch a cold and tidy up this mess you have created. After that, race back home.

3

Your mom will open the door and stare like you just came back from the depths of Hell. You won't be ready to be bombarded with questions, so push past her and head straight for the bathroom. Turn the lever handle. Water will pour into the bathtub with a roar like that of a miniature waterfall. You've always disliked the noise, but at that moment, you will embrace it. You will step in it. The sizzling bathwater extinguishes the blazing fire in your heart, but you will cry anyway.

Bitterly realize that, like Dorothy in *The Wizard of Oz*, you *must* avenge your woes. But how? Though Mrs. Lou is human, she still exceeds you in power and strength. Wait...how did Dorothy do it? Oh yes, she throws a bucket of water at the Witch, who melts afterwards...that's it! A bucket of water!

With that, a plan forms in your mind. It will thrill you to the core. After years of suppression, it's finally time for a nice little revolt. First, you will need to gather some supplies.

4

You will arrive at school the next day with food coloring and rope, ready to battle. In your ten-year-old mind, there is only one target: Mrs. Lou. The thought of her will make you want to bristle.

Review your plan again: subtly excuse yourself when the clock strikes eleven, maneuver your way to Mrs. Lou's private office, and work the setup all in under three minutes. Any longer, and you will risk detection.

Assure yourself that you've practiced the setup in your head a dozen times already, so even if your mind decides to malfunction, your body will know what to do. Now, head to your physics class and wait.

At the exact moment the clock strikes eleven, you will rise from your seat, and, in a surprisingly steady voice, ask to go to the bathroom. Your request will be granted. Exit through the front door and move noiselessly down the hallway.

The bathroom is your first stop. Refrain from cringing as the memories of yesterday invade your mind. Banish the mental images quickly. Snatch the roll of rope from the cabinet under the sink. Grab a bucket and fill it with water.

Apply the brown food coloring you found in your kitchen cabinet the night prior and mix with your hands. No one will mistake what this visual signifies, especially not Miss Sensitive herself.

Now, run towards the west wing of the school building. Make yourself as small as possible, even if you're already only five feet tall. Make a left turn, then a right, and you will find yourself standing at Mrs. Lou's office. A wave of doubt sweeps in. *What if someone sees you, Yijia? What if Mrs. Lou needs to get a folder from her office and is headed your way right now?* Stop it, Yijia.

You've done the planning and the scheming. The hard part is over. Besides, you know that Mrs. Lou has a class to teach. So, propel your legs forward with the rope gripped tightly in one hand.

Now, slip inside the office. Do not let your eyes stray. You are just looking for a chair. You will spot one near the air conditioner towards the back corner. Furrow your eyebrows. None of the classrooms have one installed even though days that are over a hundred degrees have become a common occurrence. Another reason to execute this revenge plan, you will tell yourself.

Grab the chair and haul it to the door. Lift the bucket of mushy soap firmly with both hands, step up and place the bucket carefully atop the door frame, making sure it reaches the perfect balance. Take the rope, loop one end of it through the bucket's handle, and tie a knot. Loop the other through the door handle, and tie a second knot. Make sure a perfect vertical line is formed. Now, return the chair back to where you found it, leaving no traces of your handiwork behind.

Finished, you will survey the scene with glee. When Mrs. Lou returns for lunch, she will pull on the door lever, and have her appetite fulfilled instantly. Mentally pat yourself on the back, and race back to your classroom.

Instructions for my 5th Grade Self

5

It is now Saturday, and you are at the shopping mall. The grand plan has been carried out. The echo of Mrs. Lou's shrill scream succeeding the crisp *splash* still lives rent free in your head. You know it didn't seriously change anything, but that doesn't prevent you from hoping the ice-cold water cleared that twisted head of hers a bit.

You refused to pity her as she stood there, dumbfounded, while droplets of brown liquid gliding down her arms. Now, as you pause beneath the outdoor water fountain, you will purr softly under your breath, content that Mrs. Lou has gotten a taste of the ordeal she put you through. Pray this experience resurfaces the next time she yells at you.

Stroll without a worry along the smooth marble walkway. Notice the music in the background: a harmony of gentle, flowing notes. Do not get too caught up in it, though, It's good to be on your guard at all times. Give a tight, closed-lip smile at the professional shopping guide that translates to "thanks... but no thanks". Note that he refrained from approaching you. Think about just how crazy it is that body language can convey such volumes of information.

Take that lady leaning against the wall right below the bathroom sign, for example. Watch as she listens to her companions talk, her chin out, brows furrowed, mouth slightly parted. Then, before you can avert your eyes and feign indifference, her gaze will take a ninety degree turn, meet yours for a brief second, and shift away.

Oh crap. You will gasp.

When you were six, you climbed atop a gigantic oak tree, dozed off and fell fifteen feet to the ground. The impact felt as if every wisp of air was knocked out of your throat and your brain lagged for a good second.

That is how you will feel now, as you stand, no more than twenty feet away from none other than Mrs. Lou.

You will be rooted to your spot, paralyzed. You did not expect to see your nemesis here. Then, it will register. She didn't see you. Heave a ragged breath of relief, and dare to take a closer look.

She looks completely altered. *A real life witch?* You will wonder. Suddenly magic does seem plausible. Feel your own eyes bulge more and more as they travel down Mrs. Lou's wardrobe. She has on a polka-dot printed top, some faded blue jeans, and, for God's sake, Converse? *Really?* Stare in disbelief. There is no way. Only cool, young people wear that.

Observe her surroundings. Mrs. Lou is chatting with her...friends? Blink hard. You did not think that she would have any. You can not make sense of it. Who is this woman? Watch in silent confusion as this new Mrs. Lou bursts into a loud cackle, while her face crinkles with joy. It is unlike anything you have seen or heard from her before, except perhaps that one time in second grade when Julian farted as he was giving a speech to be class president. Even then, the sound that escaped from her throat was only a half-giggle. One that stopped abruptly. One that did not reach her eyes.

Baffled by this brand new side of Mrs. Lou that you've just uncovered, you will drift towards that water fountain again.

Sit down and stare at the mixture of silver and copper circles at the bottom of the rippling water. Fumble in your purse for a nickel. Kiss it and silently wish for this new version of Mrs. Lou to become the new reality inside and outside of the classroom. Toss it in and watch as it drops towards the bottom.

About The Author

Lisa is an ardent writer who moved from China to Irvine, California in sixth grade. She loves reading, playing volleyball and exercising in her neighborhood. She hopes to spread love and joy through writing fiction, non-fiction and opinion pieces.

Instructions for my 5th Grade Self

About The Publisher

Story Shares is a nonprofit focused on supporting the millions of teens and adults who struggle with reading by creating a new shelf in the library specifically for them. The ever-growing collection features content that is compelling and culturally relevant for teens and adults, yet still readable at a range of lower reading levels.

Story Shares generates content by engaging deeply with writers, bringing together a community to create this new kind of book. With more intriguing and approachable stories to choose from, the teens and adults who have fallen behind are improving their skills and beginning to discover the joy of reading. For more information, visit storyshares.org.

Easy to Read. Hard to Put Down.

Instructions for my 5th Grade Self